Toby Alone

ROBBIE BRANSCUM

DOUBLEDAY & COMPANY, INC.
GARDEN CITY, NEW YORK

Library of Congress Catalog Number 78–22152
ISBN: 0-385-14017-7 Trade
ISBN: 0-385-14018-5 Prebound
Copyright © 1979 by Robbie Branscum

ALL RIGHTS RESERVED
PRINTED IN THE UNITED STATES OF AMERICA
FIRST EDITION

To John Schallert
Who gives me courage.
To Patty Schallert,
A beautiful lady.
To Robert Schallert,
A charmer in his own right.
And to Deborah Renae Branscum,
The flower of my life, who blooms
More beautiful each year.
And to Anna Lee and Renae Branscum,
Buds with promise.

TOBY ALONE

Other books by Robbie Branscum available from Doubleday:

JOHNNY MAY
THE SAVING OF P.S.
TO THE TUNE OF A HICKORY STICK
TOBY, GRANNY, AND GEORGE
TOBY AND JOHNNY JOE

TOBY ALONE

WITHDRAWN

South Shore High School
Port Wing, Wisconsin

1

It had been over a year since Minnie Lou Jackson had drowned, the church split up, and old Deacon Treat gone on to meet his reward. Johnny Joe Treat had been talking a year or more, too. And I do mean talking! Reckon he was trying to make up for all the years he hadn't talked at all. Fact of the matter, his always talking got on my nerves at times—even if he was my loved one, who I was going to wed come marrying time. When maybe I get sixteen in two years or a little more, for Granny didn't approve of the young marriages most Arkansas hillfolks did. Said she didn't see why folks wanted to leap into trouble, when it'd just naturally come along unaided.

Reckon I'd of wed Johnny Joe even if he hadn't learned to talk. And thinking about it, I was pure glad old Deacon Treat had gone on, and truth to tell, I bet he was a hopping and skipping over hot coals right now. Bet he was the meanest man ever. Fact, he was so rotten his meanness shocked gentle, kind Johnny Joe so's he couldn't talk. Not for years and years. And I knew no matter how much Johnny Joe talked, even if my ears fell off, I'd not say anything.

I gave a heavy sigh and looked over the farm from where I sat on the rail fence. Yep, a lot had happened in a year. Our farm was feeding us for once. Not much in winter, but in summer when garden truck was in, we lived high on the hog, Granny, George, and me.

I looked around for George, but reckoned he was out hunting for his breakfast. George is a dog. I mean, it don't matter that he thinks he's a person, he really is a dog, and he showed up on Granny's doorstep like I did. Though I had found out Jolene, Granny's youngest girl, was my ma, I never did find out where George came from. Fact was, I'd thought of myself as a bastard so long I couldn't break the habit, and called George one, too, whenever I was alone, though I'd never let Granny hear me say it.

I sighed again. It was Granny that was my worry. For some reason she had decided to get old; I mean, real old and bedfast.

Granny always looked spry and her face was the color of an apple left hanging on the tree till after first frost. I couldn't understand it; I mean, we was just getting over all our troubles when Granny just up and went to bed. I talked to Preacher Davis about it 'cause he'd known Granny since they was young'uns together.

"Not even heart-prayin' will make Granny get up, Preacher," I said worriedly.

He hitched his overall strap and looked down at me with his kind blue eyes and said, "Well, Toby gal, life has a way of slapping ye down just when ye think everything's uphill."

"Wal, it shore as shootin' knocked me on the seat of my britches," I said bitterly.

"Don't despair over yore granny, gal, she's jist bored. She was allus one fer bein' in the middle of a fuss. Reckon she don't know rightly how to take good times."

That was why I was sitting on the fence a-thinking. I had to figure some how of getting Granny up. She'd been in bed a week and I knew she was gonna die if I couldn't get her up.

"Durn ye, Granny," I muttered. "Jist cause we got us a lot of hogs, some chickens and ducks and a milking cow, and ye can have yore bellyful of greens, ye gonna die?" A feeling of impatience flashed through me and I said whispering, "Durn ye! Durn ye! Durn ye!"

I hopped down off of the fence, deciding to go over to Johnny Joe's place and talk to him. Maybe he'd have an idea.

I took the path through the woods, enjoying the coolness of fall in spite of my worry over Granny.

It was October, the month I was birthed in and the month Granny named me after. The reason most folks had forgot my real name was October, maybe it was too big a mouthful for most folks to say. 'Cause I'd been Toby ever since I could remember. Granny said I looked like fall, all brown and gold. Reckon she meant my hair and eyes coloring.

If I was October, reckon Johnny Joe was summer or spring. His hair was the color of ripe corn, his eyes sky blue, the bigness of a wide sunny summer, but the gentleness of spring.

Johnny Joe was two years older than me and nigh three times as big. But his big hands could carve delicate things from wood and just as gently set a broken leg of a squirrel or the wing of a bird. All live things were quiet and trusting with Johnny Joe. And though he had to run the big farm with just his ma and little brother and sister's help since his pa went on, he always had time for the animals and wild things of the woods.

A squirrel stood on his hind legs and scolded me for bothering him storing his winter nuts. I laughed, sticking my tongue out at him, saying, "Ye better watch how yer talkin' to me, old grandpappy squirrel, or ye'll wind up in my stewpot come winter," and laughed again as he dashed up an acorn tree.

Wild grapes dripped from vine-covered trees, and a stream gurgled softly like it was already nigh asleep for winter. I stepped high to keep from cutting my bare toes on the wet grass and weeds that grew up around the path. A fat, black snake slid slow and lazy from a sunny rock. Just about his last day before hiding out for the winter I reckoned.

A mockingbird was making a bunch of blue jays fighting mad repeating everything they said. And it was hard to believe that before many weeks passed the woods would be still and quietly sleeping under a virgin white blanket.

I saw a flash of red through the trees and knew it was George coming. There was no mistaking him, his yellow eyes, and looking like a cross between a grizzly and a lobo wolf. He come stumbling up, looking real proud of himself, so reckon he had caught himself something good to eat.

Looking at him, all the worry of Granny raised up in me and I dropped to my knees, putting my arms around his neck; I bawled like a bull calf.

"George, Granny jist don't want to stay on earth no more. Since livin' got better, she ain't even got no neighbors to talk with her 'cause they all think she's a witch woman 'cause of her doctoring and herb medicine, though they come for help fast enough when they get sick. Oh, George, I'll jist die iffen I lose Granny, ye ugly ole bastard. We ain't got nobody else. I mean, I reckon I got Johnny Joe, but we can't wed till we get growed up more. It's jist that it's allus been Granny and us."

At the sorrow in my voice, George sat back and howled, his nose pointed to the sky.

And I don't care what anybody says, that dad-blamed dog cried real tears, with his head laying on my shoulder. I wished I hadn't told that idiot about Granny a'tall, for I like to of never got him hushed. He had the whole woods in an uproar. Reckon the animals wasn't sure if something huge was coming to eat them or jist what.

When I got him quiet, I sat on a log beside the path with his head on my knees, talking to him, or maybe myself quietly. "Ye know, I jist can't understand Granny in a way, then again in a way I can. There ain't much I like better than a little excitement. I mean, it was sorta excitin' wonderin' who I was till I found out I was Jolene's—Granny's youngest girl. I reckon Granny thinks I'm all taken care of now and she can jist give up and die, but she can't, Lord, she jist can't," I said, going from thinking to praying. "I reckon, Lord, if folks wasn't afraid of Granny and the womenfolks was talkin' friendly with her, it might make her want to live. And if she could jist get spittin' mad." With that thought, I stopped still. Still as a wood thing being stalked. But my mind was spinning nine to the dozen, for I had me an idea. Maybe that's what Granny needed, to get spittin' mad.

Preacher Davis was the only close friend Granny had in our little one-room church; though she knew all the other folks well, they shied away from her in their lives. Just because Granny was good at doctoring and herb medicine, they thought she had truck with the devil.

All our lives was built around the little one-room church that was also used as the school in the few months we got to go each year. And I reckon it was from there she was going to get her will to live.

I started to grin, then said, "Lord, forgive me. I ain't right shore messin' up folks jist to get another to live is right. Fact of the matter, I'm jist about shore it's wrong, but Ye understand, Lord, it's my granny and that's why I'm askin' Ye to forgive me afore I start. But, Ye see, nobody knows Jolene is my ma and it can get nosed around that Preacher Davis jist might of fooled Granny into being my ma. After all her young'uns growed up and left.

It'll make Granny so mad it will singe the hair on her head and she'll get up fightin'. She can't abide folks lying on her. Truth to tell, Preacher Davis will be more than a mite upset. But him never bein' wed might make the stories seem real to gossip-minded folks. So, Lord, forgive me for unsettling him a mite, too, but bein' a good man, reckon he'll understand after it's over that it was for the best. Granny, I mean. Lord, jist don't never let them know I stirred up the hornet's nest, or Granny will peach-tree me till I can't set for a month of Sundays."

Somehow I'd have to figure how to get the story around so nobody would know I started it. Course I'd tell Johnny Joe. I told him everything.

But I *didn't* tell him, for when I got to their place he was staring down at a strange town girl, the daughter of his mother's friend. Smiling like he first smiled at me. Before I knowed it, life hadn't just slapped me down, as Preacher Davis said, but had clobbered me hard, right behind the ears.

2

Her name was Jamie Marlene; her lips were cherry red; her eyes, blue. Not just blue, but blue-blue; her nose was short with the sweetest little freckles ever sprinkled across it. No doubt by her own private fairy, I muttered darkly to myself. Her hair was not common. I mean no common color I ever did see, but spun silver. Not old silver, but new shiny silver. And she was fifteen and I hated her guts; and I hated that bastard George's guts, too. For he fell entirely head over clawing feet in love with Jamie Marlene's dog, Fluffy —stupid name for a dog—a small white poodle with its hair all cut and its toenails painted like the town hussies Granny had told me about. And it wore a cherry-red bow in its hair, to match Jamie Marlene's lips.

And that stupid Johnny Joe was acting like a dumb ox.

With two pairs of blue eyes on me, I shrunk into my overalls, tried to dig my toes in the dirt, and felt like I been caught buck naked, picking my nose. Shamed, jealous, and grouchy wasn't none of all I felt. Reckon a person could add pure nasty, too, to all these other feelings.

Johnny Joe acted like he hardly seen me a'tall. Just sorta absent-mindedly patted me on the head and introduced us. I forgot all about telling Johnny Joe about Granny and also forgot Johnny Joe had even fretted me for a-talking too much now that he had turned all his attention on Jamie Marlene.

George was making even more of a fool out of himself dancing around that silly-looking poodle. Standing on his back feet, his eyes half crossed, doing some sort of a courting dance, I reckon. Though I never heard of a dog doing that afore, I'd never afore seen a dog like George.

Jamie Marlene barely nodded when I said howdy. She just stared up at Johnny Joe, saying things about being so happy to stay on a real farm for a month, and that her pa might buy the farm for a summer place.

I'd never heard tell of folks having a place just for summer. Our farm was for all year, be it a butt-deep-snow winter, or sweating-hot summer. But that dumb ox Johnny Joe grinned at that city prattle like a stupid possum.

I turned sadly back down the trail home. They didn't even see me go, not even that stupid George. I hoped he danced till his dumb head fell plumb off.

There was no happiness in the woods for

me on the way home. I stopped at the church on the way and got a pencil and paper from the shoved-back desk that the teacher used when school was open. Licking the pencil I wrote on a scrap of paper, printed I mean, for I didn't want nobody to know it was my writing.

When I finished, I looked at the note, reading: "Have you ever wondered why Preacher Davis never married? Why does he visit Troyline? Why does Troyline have Toby? But Toby has no ma and pa?"

I thought the finishing touch was pretty good, if I do say so myself—"Does Toby look like Preacher Davis?" I put the note near where Mabel Horton always sat. And looking out of the church, wishing the note said, "Good-by, Johnny Joe, for a-lettin' me down for a strange girl and a durn dog with a cherry-red ribbon for a brain." Then I'd hang myself from the oak tree at the crossroads.

Tears came to my eyes as I stumbled along the dusty road toward home. My belly felt empty, but not hungry empty and I even missed George's company. But I knew I couldn't do away with me, not only because it was against God's will, but because I had to help Granny. It wouldn't be no fun to die if Granny wasn't alive to wail over me, I thought.

Oh well, tonight was prayer meeting and by Sunday the gossip would be all over the hills. Course I couldn't go to prayer meeting. Folks wouldn't expect me there, leaving Granny alone. I didn't see why the Lord couldn't let things be good all the time. I mean, it shore seemed to me we'd had enough trouble when folks had thought Preacher Davis had killed Deacon Treat and the church split up. And here was me a-starting more fuss.

Still I had to save Granny and it was the only way I knew. And I didn't let myself think where the idea might have come from. I mean up or down.

I went in and looked at Granny laying on the iron bedstead, her flannel gown buttoned up to her neck, her gray braids spread out on the pillow. Her toothless mouth seemed to have lost its firmness and the tracks of time on her face had deepened. Her small black eyes were dimmed, but strangely enough the grip of her hand seemed as strong as ever.

"Granny, be ye a mind to get up fer supper?"

"No, no, reckon not today, gal," she said, closing her eyes, tired.

Suddenly I was hopping mad clean to my toes. I mean, Johnny Joe letting me down and Granny not caring enough about me to live.

"Wal, Granny, I reckon ye don't want to eat. And why the cat-hair live for me? Go on and die!" I yelled so loud it hurt my tonsils, but I couldn't seem to stop. "Ye jist die, ye hear? It's 'cause ye don't care 'bout me. Leavin' me all by myself. Wal, go on, jist go on. 'Cause soon as yer laid in the ground I'm gonna choke George to death and then I'm gonna jump in the creek and the whole family will be gone. Then ye'll be sorry. Ye thought ye'd jist plumb die off and get some rest, didn't ye, Granny? But ye'll jist wake up on the other side of Jordan with me and old George a-starin' ye in the face. And I don't keer if the whole place goes to hell-fire."

"What ye say, gal?" Granny said, sitting up in bed fast.

"I said hell-fire and I don't see why ye keer. 'Tis a place ye ain't likely to see." My mouth dropped open and fear shot through me, for Granny hopped out of bed fast as a wink and grabbed the peach-tree switch, and bent me over a chair, setting my rear on fire, saying, "I ain't never raised a cussin' young'un, Toby gal, and I ain't a-startin' to now. Lord, forgive me for a-wantin' to go an leavin' a job not done."

The switch left a streak of fire, but I'd cuss three times a day and let Granny peach-tree my rear if it'd keep her living. When she was herself again, she sat on the edge of the bed and cried while I knelt on the floor at her feet, sobbing and taking swipes at my runny nose with the sleeve of my shirt. I wasn't crying 'cause she whipped me, though I'd of yelled like a gut-shot panther if I hadn't been so troubled on other things.

I sobbed out to Granny how lonely I'd been 'cause she was a-going off to leave me. I told her about Johnny Joe and Jamie Marlene and even how George had gone back on me. Granny's eyes flashed and the withering red-apple color was back in her face. And she begged the Lord to forgive her for a-trying to go off and leave the young'un He'd give her for comfort in her old age.

I was so glad Granny was on her feet again, and deep inside I knew it was trouble that filled her with the will to live. All her life she had been poor and had every other trouble a body could think of. Having enough to eat and such just plain bored the life out of her.

During supper (and I know Granny ate nigh a whole pot of greens and pone by herself) she snapped now, "Jist how ye gonna fight that gal and get yore Johnny Joe boy back, Toby?"

"I ain't gonna, Granny. If he wants that gal, I ain't gonna stop him. Don't want him nohow," I said, sullen.

"I ain't never raised a young'un who wouldn't fight for what was theirs," Granny snapped.

I knew that to be the danged truth. For

ever' kid she had, had fought her tooth and nail to leave home.

"Wal, I ain't got no fancy dresses like Jamie Marlene has," I muttered, mashing a bean with a fork.

"We got us some berrypicking money left, ain't we?" Granny said.

"Some, I reckon." I nodded, looking toward a fruit jar that said sassafras tea on it, knowing good and well there was twenty-three dollars in it.

"Well, I'll jist get me a ride into town with Preacher Davis, and come Sunday, ye'll have the prettiest dress in the hills, my Toby gal. Come Sunday, ye'll jist knock Johnny Joe's eyes out."

"The only way I'll knock his eye out is with my fist," I muttered under my breath. Then the word "church" seemed to scream through my head. I froze; my hair seemed to stand straight up. Good Lord in heaven! I'd tore the church up for no reason a'tall. A cussing had brought Granny back. It was too late to get to the church and tear up the note. God forgive me, poor ole Preacher Davis was gonna have to fight the devil again and this time it was me who started it. And if Granny found out, she'd not use the switch this time, she'd beat my brains out with the whole dang tree.

Granny didn't notice my fear; she was hurrying around like nothing had been worrying her and checking her supply of herb medicine.

George scratched at the door and I opened it enough in the half-light to slip outside. He started to lick at me, but pointing my finger at him, I said in a deep trembling voice, "You, you have not one true loyal bone in your sorry excuse for a body, and what's more, ye'll never, never cross this doorway again. Ye'll wander the world as the bastard ye truly are." I eased back in as George slowly slumped to the ground, more than probably in a dead faint, for he wasn't never overly brave.

I was mixed up and really feeling proud Granny was living again, but scared sick over the note I left at church and howling lonesome for my old George and Johnny Joe and seething with hate for Jamie Marlene.

For the first time in a very long time, I went to bed without mouth- or heart-praying either. My sins had suddenly piled up on me so deep it seemed there was just no starting place. And Sunday was staring me in the face like a rattlesnake ready to strike.

I tried to pray, but pictures of Jamie Marlene flashed in my head and there wasn't enough stillness or peace inside me to heart-pray.

Once when I told Preacher Davis about having trouble mouth-praying 'cause of pictures galloping in and out of my mind, he said heart-praying was a very good thing.

Now, I couldn't even do that. Seemed to me the devil had me by the tail on a downhill slide, straight to hell.

3

I closed my eyes tight, for pictures flooded behind my eyeballs so clear I shuddered. I could see Mabel Horton, her mousy brown hair in braids around her head, her breasts big and sagging to her navel. Her belly straining against her faded flour-sack dress. Her small eyes peering greedily at the note. Almost could hear her thick lips smacking.

I could see the rows of pews in the small one-room church that was used as a school also. I could see the men in faded overalls and heavy brogue shoes, holding their hats. Old folks nodding gray heads as they dozed off now and then. Young mothers proud of their squalling young'uns. Big kids on the edge of being men and women, shyly casting their eyes at each other. And Preacher Davis, the coal-oil lamplight shining on his bowed gray head, behind the pulpit, not knowing life was about to clobber him harder than it had me. And it was all my fault. I groaned and rolled in the bed like red ants were eating at me.

I wanted to run to the church and confess but couldn't, and though the fear of hellfire licked at me, I couldn't take the chance of Granny findng out what I had done. If the shock didn't kill her, the shame would. And I didn't even have Johnny Joe. I wept bitter tears of fear, self-pity, and loneliness. While outside George howled his hurt at a cold, high moon. In a way I felt a hurt for him, but seemed unable to get up and do anything about it.

I heard the rooster, Gus, warning that get-up time was nigh and must of dozed a little, for I woke to hear Granny slinging pots and pans around the kitchen. Then she was hollering, "Toby gal, get yoreself up. I want ye to go a-herb gatherin' fer me while the preacher takes me to town."

All the worries and fears of the night came piling back on me, but I knew I was safe enough on the church till Sunday, for it'd take Mabel Horton that long to spread the news that I was the love child of Preacher Davis and Granny.

A small hope hit me that maybe Mabel would count up the preacher and Granny's ages and know better. But then I knew she wouldn't, for it was just too exciting a gossip for a body to think on facts.

I sat staring at the table while Granny shoved a plate of side meat, eggs, biscuits, and gravy at me. In spite of my troubles, I ate the plate clean. So far in my life I'd never had trouble bad enough to stop me from eating. Granny once said that folks used to starving always had something to look forward to. She meant they could always eat, I reckon.

After I finished, I dragged myself out to the barn and done the chores, letting my mare, Honeysuckle, out to pasture. The trees was too thick in the woods to ride her herb gathering.

I took the milk back in the house, ignoring George who half wagged his tail while lapping up a pan of biscuits and gravy Granny had give him. For all I cared, he could have starved to death.

Granny peered at me over the dishpan of soapy water, saying, "Toby gal, ye lookin' right pale. It be yore time of the month?"

"Nigh time," I said. Not wanting Granny to fret about me.

I gathered the lard pails and headed for the woods, telling George crossly that I didn't take traitors herb gathering when he tried to follow me.

I wished the snakes hadn't gone to ground for the winter, maybe one would of bit me and then Johnny Joe would be ever so sorry! Maybe he'd spend his life crushed, living alone in the woods, thinking of what he had missed.

I jumped nigh three feet when somebody laid a hand on my head. Looking up I saw Johnny Joe smiling devilishly down at me, saying, "Little Toby, how come ye run off yesterday without sayin' yore leave-takin'?"

Anger was flashing through me again and I yanked away, saying, "Surprises me ye took note of my leavin' the way ye was bug eyein' Jamie Marlene and her silly-lookin' dog, iffen ye can call it one."

"Now, Toby honey, ye know it's a right cute little critter," Johnny Joe said sadly.

"The dog or Jamie Marlene?" I snapped and saw Johnny Joe's mouth sit firm.

"Now, Toby gal, ye know folks ought to be good to all creatures, be they human or otherwise. They's all God's."

I knew he was right, but pure poison seemed to be raging in me and pouring out of my mouth. "I reckon that girl will be yore intended wife-to-be now," I yelled, kicking at his long legs with my bare toes, but the kick hurt me worse than him. Without shoes it nigh broke my big toe. But I didn't care neither.

Johnny Joe reached out and picked me up like I was a baby and kissed me smack on the lips. I couldn't believe it. For he had never kissed me before, even knowing we was intended. It was always me climbing on a tree stump and such, to kiss him on the cheek, chin, or wherever I could reach. When he sat me gently on my feet he said sternlike, "Toby, ye know I love ye, but right now yer actin' like a dad-blamed mule."

"Will ye not talk with that girl, Johnny Joe?" I said.

"Yes, I'm gonna talk to her," Johnny Joe said. "It's common manners, Toby, to make folks welcome and I can't for the life of me figure why ye have lost yours," he flung over his shoulder as he headed toward home.

I knew he was right, but I'd seen the look in Jamie Marlene's eyes when she looked at him. And Granny had told me long ago that a man was easy addled when a gal got him stirred up below the belt buckle. Where Granny said a lot of their feeling was.

I wanted to weep and shout for him to come back, but my chin went high and hard; cold anger sat hard in me over the lump of fear of the church. Johnny Joe ought to have said he wouldn't say nothing to Jamie Marlene, I thought, for he was mine and I was his since a long time ago.

'Sides all the mess I was in was really Granny's fault for a-trying to die and leave me. Well, if I could help it, she'd never go as long as I was living. She could just face trouble with me.

I went deeper and deeper in the woods. Once I tiptoed around a small glen where Preacher Davis knelt praying. That's one thing me and him done alike. I mean, we both felt closer to God off in the woods.

It didn't take me long to fill my bucket with herbs. Granny had taught me all she knew about them long ago. But I didn't want to go home. Granny would be in town when Preacher Davis finished praying and took her, and I didn't care anything about seeing George. Anyway, he was probably over at the

Treat farm making a fool of himself over that Fluffy dog.

I found an open place by a small stream and lay on my belly in the warm fall sun, staring at the crawdads, goldfish, and tadpoles sliding colorfully across the rocky bottom of the stream—not really seeing them, for I was thinking about Mabel Horton.

It was strange how a body could know folks all their lives without knowing them a'tall. Course, I'd never thought much on Mabel one way or the other 'cept Granny never liked her much. She was always telling folks how Granny must have truck with the devil because of how Granny cured flu and all. Yet Mabel yelled for Granny loud as anybody, when it came time for her to have a birthing or sickness.

Mabel, like most of the rest of us, 'cept me, wasn't a bad person. She was just lonely. Working from sun to sun, raising eight young'uns, and putting up with a no-account drunk for a husband. She loved to get up in church at testimony time and tell how the Lord had whipped up on her husband for his sinning. Reckon it was 'cause she'd of liked to whop him herself. She liked to talk about other folks most as much as me and Granny. Somehow it made a body feel better to see another person sinning a little worse than themselves. Though Preacher Davis said it was wrong. Reckon it'd be a long, cold day in July before I'd ever see a worse person than me again.

The sun was warm on my back and I slept, making up for the wakeful night. When I woke, the shadows were creeping in on me, and grabbing my pail I ran for home. George run to me still trying to make up. I dashed past him and, sitting the pail on the kitchen table, headed for the barn to feed Honeysuckle and milk the cow, for Granny still wasn't home. It was dark by the time the eggs was gathered and I laid aside two big duck eggs for me and Granny's supper, then put two more beside them, knowing Preacher Davis would eat supper with us because he and Granny was so late getting home.

I mixed batter for a thin corn pone and stood on a chair to slice from the ham hanging from the kitchen rafters. There was two of them. The most meat me and Granny had ever had at once.

I put coffee on. And when I heard the preacher's old pickup chugging up our hill, I started frying the duck eggs.

The preacher was grinning and Granny chatting and smiling happylike as she poked a sack at me. I tried to make my face happy as I pulled out a gold-yellow dress. The gold-yellow of October. For a little, my breath caught and I was happy. Seeing me in the dress, with my gold eyes, nut-colored skin, and hair. I wanted fiercely for Johnny Joe to see me all dressed up. There was black leather shoes to go with the dress and a yellow ribbon. I flung my arms around Granny and danced her around and around the kitchen while the preacher clapped his hands and sang:

> "Hop up, Pussy-cat
>   Hop up higher
>   Hop up, Pussy-cat
>   Your tail's in the fire."

We were laughing when we sat down to eat, but Sunday flashed through me when the preacher asked the Lord's blessing on the church meeting come Sunday.

All the next day I squirmed while Granny basted up the hem of my gold-yellow dress till she snapped, "I swan, Toby, ye act like red ants got ye by the tail." It wasn't red ants, but more like the devil who had me by the tail, I thought darkly.

After the dress was fixed Granny said, "Now ye get over to the Treats and see yore Johnny Joe."

"He ain't mine," I said hateful-like.

"Now ye listen here, gal," Granny said, her black eyes snapping, "if ye stake a claim ye gotta work at it, and I didn't raise ye to give up easy. Now git."

George crept along behind me and I didn't throw rocks at him or nothing. Let him come and make a bigger fool of himself than he did the last time.

I walked around the barn just in time to see Johnny Joe lift Jamie Marlene, squealing, down from the rail fence. I wanted to turn and run, but they had seen me.

"Oh, Toby," Jamie gushed, "ye ought to have come over sooner. This big ole Johnny Joe showed me the big ole spooky woods around here. Why, I swan to goodness, there was times he nigh had to carry me, I was so scared." And she looked up, fluttering her eyelashes at him. I must say he had the grace to turn beet red and that made me feel better.

I stayed till afternoon dinner. Then it was moving toward time to go home.

Just before I stepped off the porch, a fuss like I never heard before sounded around the house. Before any of us could move, George came tearing around the house with Fluffy flying nine-to-the-dozen after him. Then I nigh died laughing, for George had Fluffy's cherry-red ribbon in his mouth. That bastard dog hadn't been untrue to me; he just wanted him a ribbon. Johnny Joe got the ribbon from George while the poodle had fits and Jamie Marlene squealed.

As soon as we got out of sight I grabbed George around the neck, and, half crying, told him how sorry I was for losing faith in him. And when we got home, I went straight in and cut him a piece of my gold-yellow ribbon for his very own.

4

George trotted, proud as a peacock, beside me and Granny, his tail sticking straight out. The golden-yellow bow sat on top of his head like a butterfly had landed there. Granny said it was the silliest fool thing she'd ever seen, but she laughed.

I wished I could of laughed and been

proud of my first real store-bought dress. My others Granny had made from flour sacking. But with church facing me, it was all I could do to keep from fainting. I kept trying to tell myself it was to help Granny and, in fact, that's why I wrote that note. But deep inside I also knew nobody had a right to cause a church trouble. For a church was beloved by God. So was Preacher Davis.

Just before I stepped in the church house I went numb. I didn't feel a thing and it was like I stood off from myself, watching me and everybody else. And if I do say it about myself, I looked mighty nice. The gold-yellow dress made my skin look like a ripe apricot, and any other time I would of loved myself. But seeing Preacher Davis standing at the door of the church, looking all loving and happy, shaking hands and welcoming flocks to God's house that he was a-taking care of, made me hurt.

I stumbled alone behind Granny, feeling about as worthless as a peach-orchard bore. Leastways Granny said peach-orchard bores were worthless 'cause their meat was stringy and tough and bitter from the stuff they ate.

I shook the hand Preacher Davis smilingly held out, feeling my heart shrivel, small and mean, and saw Mabel Horton gathered with a bunch of other women, her mouth going and a flash of paper shoved in her pocket, as she broke away from the group and headed toward Granny and me.

"I swan-to-goodness, it's good to see ye, Granny," Mabel gushed.

"Wal I do declare, Mabel, ye act like I ain't never darkened the church door afore. And I done been a-seein' ye ever Sunday and Wednesday night fer the last twenty years or so it be," Granny said, snapping suspiciously at Mabel.

"Come on, Granny," I urged, tugging at her hand, trying to drag her to the bench where we always sat. But she shook me off, cocking her ear to hear Mabel who was talking again. The other women of the church was peering at us and Mabel's voice was so loud she could be heard all over the church as she said, "I know we see each other a lot, Granny, but I was jist a-sayin' to the womenfolk afore ye come in how a body could see someone else real often and not really get to know them."

"I knowed ye. Girl and woman, Mabel Horton," Granny snapped, "and I reckon I don't want to know ye any better." And I saw Granny's face getting red, her toothless mouth clamped shut, making her nose and chin just about touch. But she held her head high as she pushed past Mabel. And now it was her dragging me to our seat.

Granny was far from stupid. She knew Mabel was backbiting her, but not why.

Then Mabel called back to Granny, "Reckon Preacher Davis knows ye better than most, wouldn't ye say, Granny?" Granny didn't answer, but her small body went straight as a poker. And all hope of confessing what I had done was gone. Heaven help Mabel Horton for smarting off. But after one look at Granny's stiff back, I knew there was nothing, nothing at all that could help me if she found out I wrote that note.

I gritted my teeth and stared straight

ahead. But hearing the whispering behind us. And when Preacher Davis rose behind the pulpit to preach, I felt the eyes burn into me as they searched for anything at all about me that might look like Preacher Davis. And to make things worse, the loving, old preacher's sermon was about folks who talked about their neighbors.

He said as how folks loved one another and that loving and caring for others was the very best thing a body could do on this green earth. And told how even money and having lots of stuff wasn't any good if folks didn't love one another.

By the time he finished, I was sicker than George the time he ran after a rabbit and caught a skunk. What made me sicker was to think Granny would of been well anyhow. I mean, just me being all tore up made her decide not to die. Lord, help me 'cause I couldn't help myself. The only thing that made life worth living at all was the way Johnny Joe stared at me openmouthed, in my gold-yellow dress, because he'd never seen me in anything but britches before.

After altar call I didn't want to "howdy" anybody, not even Johnny Joe or that simpering Jamie Marlene hanging on his arm.

I called George who was waiting nigh the pump house, still looking proud of his dumb bow. Didn't he know boy dogs ought to hate female things? Wal, I wasn't going to tell him. I'd been mean enough to him the past few days. And Lord knows I was going to need all the friends I could get, even four-legged ones.

I had my britches on and Sunday dinner started by the time Granny got home. Preacher Davis always ate with us on church day, so we fixed a big meal. I mean since our crops was good this year. Even when they was bad, the preacher ate with us, too.

"How come ye rushed off so fast, gal?" Granny asked, tying an apron around her best flour-sack dress.

"Can't abide new shoes, Granny," I said, pointing a bare toe at her.

She smiled a little but looked like she was puzzled about something, and I knew what it was. Mabel nigh openly insulted her at church.

Granny made buttermilk biscuits while I turned the chicken, sputtering in hog fat.

In spite of my trouble, that chicken looked durn good. There was a big bowl of mustard greens cooked with bacon, some of Granny's canned corn, a big bowl of butter, and a jar of persimmon butter. Granny made coffee for her and the preacher, who had come and was sitting on the porch reading his Bible till we called him to eat.

I knew the minute the preacher said grace that he knew something was wrong but, like Granny, not what. For while he was praying, he asked the Lord to help him and the church overcome anything that might keep the folks from truly worshiping in truth.

I dove into the food like it was a mother's arms and ate till I was nigh sick. I was in a sluggish stupor, but being that way was better than worrying myself to death. I staggered out on the porch and laid down beside George, who had his own troubles, for he was stuffed with leftover chicken bones and gravy.

I vaguely remember Granny and the

preacher coming out to sit in the rockers on the porch, but I was dozing off the full belly behind the old washtub full of tame honeysuckle vines. I come wide awake when Preacher Davis said, "Lord knows what the trouble is, Troyline, but I got a bad feelin' when Mabel Horton and other womenfolks called a meetin' for Wednesday night. Fer the life of me, I can't think of anything that's gone wrong in the church since Deacon Treat's death over a year ago."

"Wal, preacher, that Mabel talked right pert to me this mornin'," Granny said. "Sorta put my back up, she did."

"Wal, Troyline, I reckon the devil hates to see a church doing as well as ours has been, so he's a puttin' somebody to cause trouble." With that I slid off the porch and around the house, headed for the barn.

I called Honeysuckle, my mare. I didn't need a bridle or saddle 'cause I could guide the mare anyway I wanted her to go with my knees. And I reckon it must of been I wanted to see Johnny Joe because that was where we wound up without me really noticing where I was going.

What surprised me, and made me happy for the first time in days, was Johnny Joe being almost rude to Jamie Marlene. I mean, the rudeness didn't make me happy, but Johnny Joe saying he wanted to talk to me alone. And taking the mare's mane, he led us to the barn lot, leaving Jamie Marlene sitting on the porch with her mouth open.

When we reached the barn lot Johnny Joe yanked me off Honeysuckle, none too gently, and held me about three feet off the ground, staring me eyeball to eyeball, saying grimly, "Now lookie here, Toby, ye been actin' like a cat with its tail caught in a crack, and since I'm gonna marry ye, ye best tell me what's ailin' ye. And, Toby, ye looked larpin' good in yore gold-yéller dress." With that he sat me down on a stump, and bawling like a bull calf, I told him all. I mean about me wanting Granny to live and the note I'd wrote so's Granny would get mad enough to live. And how Granny had already got up before the note was found.

I sniffed and swiped my nose on my sleeve. There was dead quiet, and I nigh fainted when I looked up and saw Johnny Joe's face. His eyes were flashing blue flame at me and his big hands were clenching and unclenching. I'd never seen Johnny Joe mad before, and I could feel the hair raising on the back of my neck and took a slant-eyed look to see how far I'd have to run if I decided to make a dash for Honeysuckle.

Johnny Joe must have seen the look in my eyes, for his big hands came down hard on my shoulder and his eyes burned into mine. His voice was hard as he said, "Toby, ye lissen and heed me good. I don't blame ye fer a wantin' yore granny to live, but how in this world ye could stir up a whole church and hurt a good man like Preacher Davis I'll never understand. Now ye get right home and tell yore granny and Preacher Davis, too." I shook my head no. Johnny Joe didn't understand; if I told Granny what I'd done, I'd have to tell the whole church. And after Granny had beat me to death, she'd lay down and die. There wasn't no way out that I could see.

"Toby, are ye gonna do what I tell ye?" Johnny Joe asked me.

I shook my head, stubbornly, no again.

Suddenly Johnny Joe was turning me every way but loose. He picked me up and in mid-air flipped me over his knee and, I swan-to-goodness, whopped my rear. And I swan-more-to-goodness I was sick and tired of getting my rear whopped. It felt on fire where his big hand had slapped. And hate flew from my toes to my ears. Wild, killing thoughts flew through my mind. I even wished I was pregnant by him so the spanking would make me miscarry so he'd be forever sorry, but that wasn't likely since we'd never done nothing. Nor was apt to before being wed. But now I wasn't even going to wed him.

I turned and twisted trying to get away, but I didn't argue or ask him to quit. I'd die afore I did. I tried to move my leg so he'd hit it instead of my butt. Maybe he'd break my leg and I'd never walk again. I'd be an old lady dressed in black, sitting in a chair all my life. And Johnny Joe'd be so sorry, he'd never wed and wait on me all my life to make up for what he'd done.

With a last hard whack, he sat me on my feet. I felt my whole body was blazing hate at him, and I said, "Listen, Johnny Joe Treat, I'll never ever wed the like of ye. Hittin' a person littler than ye ain't fair. Ye can jist have that stupid Jamie Marlene. Ye ain't got no right a-tellin' me what to do."

Johnny Joe reached for me and I do believe that dang ox had tears in his eyes. I always knew he couldn't abide hurting things. And, if I was truthful, knew it was my meanness, turning on Jamie Marlene and hurting Preacher Davis, that drew him to it, but I was too mad and hurt myself to care. No matter what I'd done, it didn't give him no right to whop up on me.

Johnny Joe took a step toward me, but I whirled and ran. Taking a flying leap I was on Honeysuckle's back, my hands in her mane and my knees clamped to her sides. I had come here for comfort and got whipped for my trouble.

Sitting on the mare, looking at the anger dying out of Johnny Joe's face, I went plumb stark-raving crazy.

5

With something between a gut-shot panther and a rebel yell, I dug Honeysuckle in the ribs and we took the farm-lot fence almost from a standing leap. I heard Jamie Marlene scream and Johnny Joe yell, but I never stopped and looked back.

I rode Honeysuckle hard, but not as hard

as the devil was riding me. I'd started out to make Granny want to live and had messed up not only my life but Granny's, Preacher Davis', and Johnny Joe's.

I flew past Clem Jackson's place, feeling glad that pore ole Johnny Joe would never know the joy of having me, Toby, for his wife. And his spanking me decided that; for no woman worth her salt would let a husband whip her, let alone afore they wed.

By the time we got to Big Creek it was getting late and the October sun was losing its warmth. I rubbed Honeysuckle down with dry grass and let her drink her fill from the creek, a little at a time. She acted so feisty I knew she could of run twice as far.

It was dark by the time I got home and Granny didn't say anything as she rushed the chores. Reckon her thoughts was still on the strange way the womenfolk acted at church that morning.

We didn't go to church that night. Granny grumbled about being too old to climb the rocky path in the dim lantern light. I looked at her sharply, for Granny had never complained of being old before. She did look tired. Some of her sparkle gone.

Fear smote me. "Dear Lord, don't take Granny on," I heart-prayed. "Oh, Lord maybe Granny is tired of living." Well, it was shore I'd know by Wednesday night when the church meeting was called. It seemed a hundred years till Wednesday-night prayer meeting and yet like it was coming fast as a falling star on a hot summer night.

I moped around, just doing what I had to. Granny kept asking me if my time of month was on me and I lied and said yes so's she wouldn't fret. She wanted to know if I'd made it clear to Jamie Marlene that Johnny Joe was my marrying man and I said yes to that, too.

My time of the month wasn't on me, but I felt the cares of mine and Granny's world was. Seemed every day Granny's step got slower and the tracks of time deeper in her face. And I got over feeling guilty for the note I had written; for after watching Granny, I knew it was going to take a good fight to keep her going. And though I knew it was wrong and I hated to hurt Preacher Davis, I'd do it double to keep my granny going.

My heart hardened toward Johnny Joe and I told myself I no longer cared what he thought of me. One thing for sure, he now knew that this was one Toby gal who didn't take kindly to spanking. But truth to tell, my not loving Johnny Joe left a mighty empty hole in my belly.

One thing, me and George got closer and closer. I could just about nigh sit and howl at the moon with him. And would have if I hadn't been a-feared Granny would hear me.

George is a good dog but apt to get uppity if you pay too much mind to him, but I did think he'd help me and Granny all he could when danger came if he was sure he wouldn't get hurt.

I knew for a fact I lost my mind the day Johnny Joe spanked me, but the odd thing was I never knew one day from the next what form my craziness would take. One day I'd prowl the woods with George, stopping to cry in his shaggy coat once in a while. Another day I dogged Granny's steps, staring at her like I'd never seen her before till she threatened to peach-tree me if I didn't get out of her way.

On Wednesday, my doomsday, I got up raving hungry. I cooked and ate all day, biscuits, eggs, gravy, and cups and cups of coffee sneaked behind Granny's back. For she didn't hold with young'uns drinking coffee till they was wed.

At noon I ate plate after plate of beans, corn bread, raw onions, and drank a glass of buttermilk. Granny said, "I swan, Toby, is yore time of month on ye again?" I just nodded yes and kept eating. I could hardly drag out on the porch afterward. But by midafternoon I was starving again. Seemed my whole world had just narrowed down to what I could taste. Granny lay down to rest up for church and I knew she was going to need it more than she did.

I mixed up a batter of flour, eggs, vanilla, and milk and pan-fried the sweeting bread in round, crisp cakes and ate them sprinkled with sugar and gobs of butter till I was nigh drunken sick. And still my belly felt empty. And at supper I stuffed myself again and was so full and miserable I didn't much care if I was walking or flying on the way to church.

My mind had gone plumb back on me and once in a while I found myself absently singing or humming like I was the happiest person in the world.

There was more folks than usual in prayer meeting, so I knew word had spread. Preacher Davis was looking puzzled, but welcoming folks with "God's blessing ye," to everybody that shook his hand. Granny perked up a mite at all the folks' eyes on her, but I noticed she hurried to sit down, like she was powerful tired.

When folks quieted down a mite, Preacher Davis rose from behind the pulpit and asked God's blessing on the meeting that had been called, then he pinned Mabel Horton with his eyes and said, "Ye wanted a meetin', Mabel, so ye jist trot up here and tell us what's on yer mind. 'Cause God's house belongs to us all and we're all free to have our say." Preacher Davis then sat down and

Mabel, her face red with importance, flustered her way up behind the pulpit, saying, "Now, Preacher, ye know I do hate trouble and fuss and the Lord knows I hate sad tidings, but there's been terrible secrets a-goin' on right in front of our noses and for at least fifteen years that we know of. And the good folks in this church is mighty concerned that it be put a stop to."

The preacher had uncrossed his legs and was leaning forward, his ears cocked like a hound-trailing coon. Granny's eyes glittered up at Mabel, who stuttered to a stop. "Wal, out with it, Mabel, what and who is doing this awful secret thing yer talkin' on?" the preacher prodded her.

"'Tis ye and Troyline over yonder," Mabel busted out, pointing her finger at Granny, and Granny's back went straight and her chin shot up five inches.

"What in cat-hair ye rattlin' about Mabel?" Granny snapped. "What secrets I been a-doin' out of the ord'nary?"

"Ye and Preacher Davis, Troyline, that's who. I got it on good fact that ye and

Preacher Davis has been a-carryin' on behind our backs fer years. And that Toby gal thar is yores and the preacher's."

"What!" Granny yelped, jumping straight up from her seat. And Preacher Davis looked like he'd been struck by lightning.

"Mabel Horton, has something cracked that peanut brain of yourn?" Granny yelled. "Why, me and Preacher Davis been friends fer years, and goodness knows we ain't never even kissed."

"Ye don't have to kiss to get a young'un, Troyline. And goodness ain't got nothin' to do with it!" Mabel snapped.

Granny drew herself up straight and cold, saying, "The good Lord knows the truth, Mabel Horton. I know who Toby's folks be, but I ain't never gonna tell ye and yore like who they be!" Granny thundered.

"Ye can screech all ye like, Troyline," Mabel screamed. "But facts be facts, and the preacher ain't never sat his feet under other folks' dinner table as much as he has yores, Troyline, so reckon he been gettin' more than fried chicken at yore place."

Granny was so mad she sputtered, and Preacher Davis was trying to get folks quiet, for the whole church was muttering and twisting around. All but me. I was waiting for the Lord to strike me down for sinning.

Preacher Davis shoved Mabel Horton aside none too gently and pounded on the wooden pulpit till people quieted down and, glaring at the now scared Mabel, said, "Sit!" And Mabel scurried to her seat, looking like she was scared she'd went too far. And I felt sorry that I had got her in such a bad way. I mean, leaving the note where she could find it.

"Now I don't know whar ye all got this idee about me and Troyline, but they ain't no truth in it, and that's the Lord's truth."

I felt my hair raise on the back of my neck and without looking knew it was Johnny Joe glaring at me. I slid further down in my seat and Preacher Davis went on, "I'm surprised and sorry to think my people would believe the devil's work. Troyline has been my friend for too many years to count and the Lord knows there ain't nothin' bad to hide. Toby ain't my young'un, though I'd of been right proud to have a gal like her." (Ye wouldn't neither, I thought bitterly.) Then the preacher said, "I'm too old now to change my spots, and iffen ye all can believe such backhanded doin' of me, I reckon I best give up this here church here and now."

My heart seemed to crack as the preacher bowed his old gray head and stumbled back from the pulpit.

"Ye ain't gonna do no such thing, Preacher," Granny's voice cracked across the room. And like a small blackbird she was up on the stage beside the pulpit, facing the church folks. Her eyes were snapping and her voice loud and clear as a bell. "Mabel Horton, I'm plumb ashamed of ye. I mean ye being so fast to place sins on other folks. Lord have mercy, woman can't ye figger? I was eighty-two summers come the last one and was plumb past birthin' years afore Toby was born. And this good man here ye been bad-mouthin' is true and good and faithful only to God his father. He ain't had, or never will have, no time fer womenfolks other than jist pure Christian love."

Before Granny could say anything else, the folks caught what she meant about her age and a low titter turned into loud belly laughs. And I saw poor Mabel shrink before my eyes, her importance gone and her eyes not understanding how she could turn into a sudden figure of fun. To be mocked by the very folks that had joined her in the back talk about the preacher, Granny, and me.

Suddenly I was on my feet, saying, "Ye all hush and heed what I say." The folks fell quiet so sudden my ears hurt. My guts twisted in a knot, but I went on, "My granny allus told me to tell the truth and shame the devil, but instead I told lies and shamed the Lord, I reckon. I ain't got no good excuse 'cept my granny has been a-wantin' to die and I ain't been a-wantin' her to, so I figured if I wrote some gossip on a piece of paper and left it for somebody to find, namely Mabel Horton, trouble would start and Granny would get mad enough to want to live, and that's the simple truth of the matter, and it's right sorry I am, Preacher Davis. I ask you, the church, and most of all God's pardon for causin' a fuss, but my granny allus did like a good fuss."

Even before hearing the tiny thump, my heart cold, I turned to see Granny laying on the plank floor like a small bird that had been shot down in mid-flight. Oh, dear Lord, in trying to make my granny want to live I've killed her, my mind screamed, as I knocked and shoved people right and left to get to my granny, my mother, my father, my teacher, my dear granny's side. And just as I reached her, a dog sent up a long, lost howl to the blackness of the night sky. And somewhere in the back of my mind I knew it was George, with his stupid-looking gold-yellow ribbon in his shaggy hair.

6

It was Johnny Joe who carried Granny home. I stumbled ahead carrying the lantern, lighting his path the best I could. Preacher Davis walked slow and old, behind; and George sobbed and whimpered alongside Johnny Joe.

It was a strange world I walked in. Empty and cold. The huge October moon showed an unsmiling face and the stars glittered like ice on a blue, cold morning. My whole insides were as empty and cold as the mist.

When we got home, Johnny Joe lay Granny on the bed while I undressed her and put on her gown. Preacher Davis and Johnny Joe lit all the lamps and built a fire in the fireplace and the kitchen stove. Somebody put a pot of coffee on.

I rubbed Granny's hands over and over, waiting and waiting for her to open her eyes. And when she did, at first she didn't seem to know where she was. Then she saw me and Granny smiled, "Toby gal, call the preacher. I'm a-gonna go see my maker and don't ye have no fits, gal, 'cause I got things to take keer of." I just nodded numbly. "Call the preacher!" Granny said in a voice that didn't sound like it was a-dying, but her face was white and tired.

Preacher Davis came and took one of Granny's hands, and Johnny Joe stood at the foot of the bed.

"I know a-preachin' my funeral will be

hard on ye, Preacher, I mean as us a-bein' such close friends and all," Granny said, "but I don't hold with a stranger talkin' over me about things he don't know nothin' of."

"Ye know I wouldn't let no stranger talk over ye, Troyline," the preacher said gently. "And do ye want to be buried next to yer man?"

"Cat-hair no!" Granny snapped. "Couldn't abide that man livin' and shore couldn't stand him dead."

"We have shore had us some times, ain't we, Preacher?" Granny said smiling. "We doctored folks and buried some; fought some and loved some."

"We shore have had good times, Troyline, and when we meet on the other side we'll have even better times because we'll be with God our Father."

"Amen, Preacher," Granny said softly. "Now let me speak to Johnny Joe, and, Preacher, reckon ye can have that thar kiss from me. The one that ye tried to steal too many years ago to count." The preacher stooped and gently kissed Granny on the lips before stepping back to let Johnny Joe take his place.

I suddenly realized that the preacher and Granny had loved each other. Loved each other long and deep. Then reckoned maybe Granny was right, I mean when she said Preacher Davis loved God more than womenfolks. Maybe he figured he couldn't put God first if he had a woman to worry on. Knowing Preacher Davis and Granny, I knew that even though they loved, their honor code had never let them go beyond friendship. And if I could of felt pain, I reckon the pain of their loving, yet never touching, would have killed me on the spot.

"Johnny Joe," Granny said, and her voice seemed to falter then got strong again, "I'm right glad Toby has a fine man like ye to wed. She's a good gal but a little hardheaded, I reckon, but ye could never find no better. I couldn't abide her not bein' loved, so take care ye do." Johnny Joe just smiled gently into Granny's eyes, and Granny nodded.

"Now, Toby, come close, gal," Granny said. And the room and people faded out; it was just Granny and me. "Oh, Toby, Toby," Granny said, holding my hands tight. "Ye were the last flower of my youth and the most beautiful, I reckon. Ye're might hurt now, young'un, but Granny's old and tired, but once, Toby gal, I was young like ye. I was Troyline and I roved the woods and hills. Troyline, Toby, Troyline not Granny. I've had good times and bad, and even the bad times was good if ye can understand that, Toby. Toby, I ain't a-leavin' ye 'cause I want to, gal, but 'tis time and I be right glad to rest in the arms of my maker. But, Toby, I ain't a-really leavin' ye, gal. Why, most everythin' around is a part of me. The blood in yore veins, the hills and woods, the herbs ye'll be gatherin' when I'm gone; the medicine ye'll make fer the sick folks is my teachin', Toby gal.

"Toby gal, don't look like that. Let me rest, child. Life has been a long, hard trip, and oh, child, it's not death in sight, but blessed rest! Old friends who've gone on along, and kinfolks, though I reckon a bunch of them went t'other way. I'll find out who soon enough," Granny said, looking suddenly eager to hurry on.

I could 'most see her nosing around heaven trying to find out stuff on other folks.

Preacher Davis tried to ease out the door once to get the doctor, but Granny called him back saying 'twas no use.

"Now, Toby, I want ye to lay me out. 'Cause I don't want no womenfolks a-sayin' I wasn't clean or tellin' others I had a strange mole on my body or somethin'. Probably say I had horns." Granny's voice ran on, fussy. "I want ye should wrap me in the honeysuckle quilt afore shuttin' me in the box, and just bury me in my gown. Ain't no sense a-wastin' good cloth noways. Ye bury me under the cedar by the pond. Though after I'm gone, I reckon it won't matter if ye throw me in it. 'Cept I might pizen the water in it." Granny tried to chuckle but coughed instead.

Her grip tightened on my hands and she rose a little from the pillow. "Oh, Toby, Toby, my October baby, we done loved, gal, and the love'll stay with us both 'cause love never dies, Toby. That's how come God is love. Ye stay close to Him, Toby, He'll never leave ye. He's never left me in all my years, and He's a-waitin' now. Toby, don't ye feel bad 'cause of the trouble at church tonight. The Lord knows ye meant well and 'twas not a bad fuss, gal. Reckon Mabel would have met her match iffen I hadn't of been dyin'." Granny's eyes were fading and her voice. I held on as hard as I could and jumped when Granny suddenly said, "They's folks a-waitin', Toby gal. I can 'most see their faces—Wal, I swan, Homer, I never dreamed I'd see ye up—" Granny's voice whispered away and she fell limp against her pillow.

Gently, Preacher Davis closed her eyes. And more gently, Johnny Joe pulled me away, into his arms. But, dry-eyed, I shoved him away.

I put water on to heat for Granny's bath, and the menfolks went outside while I bathed her small body and put her newest flannel gown on her. I combed her hair and braided it neatly, and felt nothing. Nothing at all. I could hear Johnny Joe down at the barn building Granny's box.

Preacher Davis tried to get me to lay down. But I started planning, for Granny, my Granny, was going to have the best funeral ever. Years later, folks would say they'd never ate so well as at Granny's burying.

"Who's Homer?" I asked, not really caring.

Preacher Davis sat his coffee cup down with a trembling hand and chuckled. "He was the meanest bootlegger around the hills when me and Troyline was young'uns. Reckon he must of changed more than a mite since them days."

"Reckon so, Preacher, if he's dead," I said dryly.

I put the two hams me and Granny had been saving for winter on to boil a while before baking and told Preacher Davis to take my bed and rest 'cause it was better for me to work. He didn't back talk, just laid his hand on my head and said, "They's many ways of grievin', Toby."

I didn't tell him I wasn't grieving. I wasn't nothing at all but giving Granny the best send-off I could.

By sunup I had stacks and stacks of pies. Apple from our cellar, pumpkin, raisin, and berry cobblers. I had yellow egg cakes and molassed-flavored cakes. And as the morning went on, I added potato salad in huge bowls. I opened jars and jars of pickles and relishes that Granny and I had canned.

Johnny Joe carried Granny's fresh-smelling pine box in and, without a word between us, we wrapped her in her honeysuckle quilt and lay her in it. And sat the box across two straight-backed chairs in the living room.

Johnny Joe took a look around the kitchen and stared at me, then went out the door to kill chickens to fry. He who loved all live things. He knew, without saying, that I was giving Granny the best send-off I could.

I fried platters of chicken and it never crossed my mind that I was fixing up the food me and Granny had been saving for winter. It didn't matter, now that Granny was gone.

I took the huge, sugar-crusted hams out of the oven and filled the pan they were in with sweet potatoes to bake. The table and sideboard sagged with food, and the stove was loaded, too. Finally Johnny Joe put some planks across chairs and I filled them up, too.

The Preacher and Johnny Joe ate and drank some coffee. And by that time folks were coming in. All the folks, folks who didn't even go to church, but folks Granny had doctored. The house filled and flowed out in the yard. Johnny Joe and some of the menfolks built tables with planks outside. And all who came brought food.

I worked and worked and smiled and smiled. Overhearing one woman say, "Land sakes, I never seen a young'un act like that Toby girl. She's a-turnin' down all offers of help."

I didn't care. I just went on. Stopping now and then to go peek at Granny.

When night came, I shocked folks even worse 'cause I said nobody was a-going to sit up with Granny but me and George. Folks started to protest angrily, saying dogs didn't sit up with passed-on folks, but Preacher Davis got them quiet by saying, "Let be. Jist let Toby be."

Some of the folks went home to return

the next day. But most stayed, talking low and putting babies to sleep on pallets.

The living room was quiet, with a coal-oil lamp turned low, Granny sleeping and me and George sitting.

"Who's in thar?" I heard someone ask and Johnny Joe gently reply: "Why it's just Toby, Granny, and George."

7

It ain't nobody's never mind what I said to my granny and George that night. 'Sides, I couldn't rightly recall, but I do know for a fact George never once closed his eyes.

It was early when the preacher and Johnny Joe came for Granny. For a spell I wanted to hang on her box and not let her go, but I didn't and the numbness came back.

Me and George followed the folks and stood back alone as the preacher said farewell to Granny. And they buried her under the cedar tree.

Folks for miles around said, "Toby, ye done give your granny the best send-off a body could give." And I nodded and smiled as they ate their way through the stacks of food far into the day. Preacher Davis and Johnny Joe didn't want to leave till I told them softly to leave me be.

After they left, I cleaned and cleaned some more, talking lost to George who followed me every step, carrying a huge bone in his mouth like he was afeard I'd take it back.

It was night again and Johnny Joe came back. The house was shining clean and the leftover food in the cellar to keep. It was the third night since I'd slept and couldn't remember when I last ate. Somehow my body kept moving. And I didn't answer Johnny Joe when he tried to reason with me. "Toby, ye best rest. Have ye eat yet? Listen, Toby, ye best talk to me." Suddenly he slapped me so hard my head snapped around, and a deep trembling started at my toes. I shook so hard my teeth rattled together.

"Oh, yer brave, ain't ye?" I screamed at Johnny Joe. "A-slappin' a body littler than ye. Wal, it don't take no three times to know what kind of man ye be. First a-whoppin' my rear, now a-slappin' me over."

Johnny Joe protested he was only trying to help me. I screamed him plumb out of the house. When he was gone I fell across Granny's bed and hugged her pillow. Johnny Joe said later that I slept for two days and nights. And he fed George and done my chores.

I said coldly that I thanked him, but I would like for him to leave. He looked down at me with tears in his eyes, but they didn't move me at all. I just wanted to be alone. Just me and George.

Some place deep down I was a little sad that Johnny Joe was going to miss out on me being his wedded wife. And figured Jamie Marlene wouldn't suit him nigh as good as me, and that made me feel a little good. But I didn't need, nor want, folks close to me. They'd just die and leave me like Granny done. 'Sides, sometime during my long sleep I'd decided to be a real herb-woman doctor like Granny. I'd let folks think I was a witch, but I'd help them with medicine.

I ate for the first time in days and was sure surprised to find nigh all our winter food gone and the leftovers in the cellar had all spoiled, and I had to feed it to the hogs 'cause hogs will eat anything and poison won't hurt them. They even eat rattlesnakes.

I spent the day going through Granny's herb medicine, seeing what we was low on that I'd need to fix up before the long, blue-cold winter set in. One thing sure, I was going to live alone with George and never, never love no one ever again.

I spent my days roving the woods, digging and picking herbs and boiling and seeping them into medicine and storing them. Granny had taught me to make syrup for coughs, for cold rubs, and all sorts of ailments.

I fed, cared for, and talked to the animals on the farm, and ducked behind bushes, trees, and most any place, hiding from Johnny Joe when he came to call.

Two weeks passed with me hiding from Johnny Joe, when Preacher Davis come to call, for I had quit church, too. Truth to tell, I nigh broke down when I saw his old gray head and kind, faded eyes, and Granny seemed close while he was there. But he didn't look so kind when I told him I wasn't never going to no church no more.

"Toby, yer actin' plumb sinful," he snapped. "Iffen yore granny was here, she'd peach-tree the seat of yore britches."

"Ain't nobody gonna hit me no more, Preacher," I said coldly.

"Glory be, young'un, Troyline would turn over in her grave iffen she could hear ye talkin' that-a-way."

"Then she oughta stayed on with me," I said flatly.

"Toby, ye ain't dumb. When a body's gotta go, they got to go."

"But they don't have to want to!" I yelled. "Granny wanted to go."

"Toby, Troyline was tired and old. She loved ye, gal, better than most anybody, but,

Toby, her body jist plumb wore out. Like mine and even yours will years from now."

"Preacher, ye can talk all ye want, it jist won't do any good 'cause I ain't never gonna love nobody again, then I won't care if they pass on."

"Toby, ye can't hide from life, and death is part of livin'. We jist do the best we can while we're here and be ready to go when the time comes."

"Wal, Preacher, I don't want to go and it don't seem fair that we are made to whether we want or not. And if I could help it, I'd not ever leave this world."

"But, Toby, ye can't help it, young'un. 'Sides, in the other life we'll live forever."

"I want to live here forever, Preacher," I said stubbornly.

Preacher Davis shook his old head sadly and walked off, saying, "I'll be a-prayin' fer ye, Toby gal."

I wanted to feel sad that I had hurt him, but I couldn't.

After that, folks left me alone 'cept coming for the medicine I brewed when sickness come.

Nearly every day I caught sight of Johnny Joe either walking by the house or slipping through the woods.

Sometimes I forgot to eat for a day or two and other times George and me would eat a whole fried chicken between us. Sometimes I spent hours by Granny's grave telling her what kind of herbs I'd been getting and who had been sick and what kind of medicine I'd given them. I told her all the gossip I could find out while visiting sick folks. I mean, like one of the Satterfield girls having a young'un without being wed. And how the baby looked a lot like Clem Jackson to me. For my granny ever did like a good gossip.

Sometimes when things in the hills were too quiet, too still, I'd tell Granny for hours just why I was not going to marry Johnny Joe. And at other times I'd get a feeling Granny would just as soon I'd hush and go about the business of living. When that feeling come on me, I'd scoot for the house or woods. Alive, Granny had a wicked switch hand, and my hair stood on end thinking what she might do, and her dead.

First frost came and I gave Mr. Bates a ham and side of pork for killing one of our hogs, 'cause me and George would need winter meat.

Every day the frost got heavier and heavier like a baby snow. I had to start wearing shoes. George still wore his gold-yellow ribbon, though it was mostly strings from him getting it caught in bushes, chasing rabbits and things, but he growled if I tried to take it off.

Seemed without me knowing it, I got more interested in herb medicine every day. And without knowing it, I got pure enjoyment out of doctoring folks and nosing in their lives. When I was at their houses, some of the womenfolk would say, "I swan, Toby, 'tis like havin' yore granny back."

When backwoods folks acted a mite scared of me 'cause of my herb doctoring, I liked that, too, and tried to act as witchie as I could. Without ever having seen one that I knew of.

I really liked getting new babies in the

world and easing the pain of old folks, for the town doctor was far away, and 'sides, folks couldn't have paid him even if he could of found his way around in the woods.

As winter came on I was busy as I could be. There was days I didn't get to visit Granny's grave, for the winter started out with sickness and I'd be miles away by sunup, me and George.

If I thought I couldn't get home in time to feed the stock and milk the cow, I'd hang a cloth on Clem Jackson's gatepost, and he'd take care of the chores for me, keeping the milk and eggs of that day for his trouble.

I had more patients than Granny, for Granny had been too old to go as far afield as me. Sometimes I rode Honeysuckle but mostly I walked, for some of the people didn't have enough feed for her, and lots of times not enough for me or themselves. In these cases I took them food and in other cases folks paid me in food. So it worked out all right. I mean, me and George had plenty of food at home—duck eggs and such.

I was getting Mabel Horton's daughter,

Olie, hot-pepper tea to ease her labor pains, when the first heavy snow of winter began to fall. By morning there was a new baby boy in the house and a deep snow on the ground.

Me and George waded home, carrying side meat and a peck of corn meal that I would later take to old Grandma and Grandpa Stevens that was too old to work and was having a hard time of it.

I was passing the old Odom place, just on this side of Johnny Joe's, when I came to a dead stop, staring at the newly cleaned-up house and yard. I come fully alive with a jolt, for that silly white poodle, Fluffy, with a cherry-red ribbon in her hair, run across the yard, yelping at me and George. And Jamie Marlene was giggling right behind her.

8

"Oh, Toby, Toby, whar ye been ever so long?"

A hot flash of red jealousy shot across my brain and my whole body was in shock. I had thought I didn't love Johnny Joe anymore, but the sight of silver-haired Jamie Marlene made me realize I'd nigh lost my life mate.

"Lord a mercy, Granny, I done nigh lost Johnny Joe," I thought to myself. Steadying my lips in what passed for a grin, I said, "Ah reckon I been too busy to visit much. 'Sides I thought ye was only stayin' a month."

"Oh, Toby, didn't ye know we done moved here from town?"

"Ye don't say?" I said, to keep from cussing fierce.

"Oh yes. Ma and Pa wanted to be nigh me after I was wed."

"Ye be wed?" I asked sharper than I intended to, but Jamie didn't seem to notice.

"Why, didn't ye know, Toby, that Johnny Joe has spoken fer me?"

My head seemed to rip apart and slam together again. From somewhere a cool, clear voice said, "Wal, that's right nice, Jamie Marlene." And I walked on old, old as Granny, toward home. Out of Jamie Marlene's sight, my feet picked up speed till I was running, sliding through the snow. Wet and cold outside and raging inside. I was feeling every feeling a body could feel. I was no longer numb, and my granny was gone. I'd lost Johnny Joe and turned Preacher Davis against me for the mean way I'd acted toward him and the church.

I took my gold-yellow dress off its nail and laying with it across Granny's bed, I cried; not just cried but wailed out all my lonely sorrow. George came whimpering up and I yanked him upon the bed and, burying my face in his coat, sobbed and talked, "Oh, George, I went plumb crazy when Granny passed on, thinkin' I never wanted a body close no more. It ain't so! It ain't so!" I howled so loud it shamed me quiet, and in my mind I heard Granny's voice saying, "Toby gal, I ain't never raised no addled young'un till now. If ye'd start a-growin' up and goin' about yer business 'stead of bawlin' over spilt milk and stop a-grumblin' around my restin' place 'stead of livin' the way ye was taught, ye wouldn't be in this fix now. I know I raised ye with grit and backbone. Why don't ye do somethin' about yore troubles, Toby gal, and let me rest?"

"I will, Granny, I will," I whispered.

"And, Granny, I'm right sorry I was mad when ye went off and left me."

George brought me out of my thoughts by squirming out of my grip. I got up, swiped my nose with the sleeve of my shirt, and said out loud, "Granny, I ain't a-sayin' good-by to ye 'cause, like ye said, love don't never die, but I'll let ye rest, and, Granny"—I laughed out loud—"I know and ye know it ain't proper, but I'm a-goin' a-courtin'."

It might have been the wind in the pine tops, but it shore sounded like Granny's heh heh laugh to me.

I took off my wet britches and put on my flannel gown and took a big swallow of Granny's homemade medicine. Just in case the cold and wet might try to give me a cough. Then I sat on George's back and poked some down him. 'Cause I didn't want him a-getting sick on me.

Since Granny's medicine was a good deal corn whiskey, it didn't take me or George long to get to feeling better. For the first time since Granny passed on, I felt like me—Toby, Toby, Toby, Toby! I half singsonged around the house. A sore, tired, beat-up Toby, but it was good to be me again. If now and then a nagging worry slipped in, asking whether I was right sure I could get Johnny Joe back, I laughed it off, for Granny's blood flowed in my veins, and I'd never all of my life saw her give up. 'Cept when she passed on, and since I'd come to myself, I knew she couldn't help that.

For the first time in what seemed years, I was feeling deep about Johnny Joe again. And I knew he'd be my forever and always love. It would be a shame if he missed out on wedding me 'cause there was nobody in the world who could love him like I did. I was just plumb crazy for a spell. I hadn't never stopped loving, just went numb, and somehow I'd have to get Johnny Joe to understand that.

The tingle of battle heated my blood and I was happy again, which made George happy, for he got a hambone with meat still on it.

I slept good, without dreams, and woke up with an urge to get my courting underway, but knew I had to make things right with Preacher Davis. So after chores, I called George and we headed for the preacher's house by the church.

The sky was dark and heavy with snow clouds, but in my heart the sun was shining. I carried a bottle of Granny's cold medicine for the preacher. Wind blew cold and icy through the treetops, blowing hunks of snow from the limbs; and me and George had to duck and dodge to keep from getting clobbered.

The preacher's face lit up when he saw me and he acted like he'd never seen me being mean at all. He led me to his kitchen, more spotless than any woman's, and gave me a cup of sweet coffee that was most milk, but good and hot.

Granny always said it was best to grab the bull by the horns, so looking him straight in the eye, I said, "Look-a-here, Preacher, I done ye a bad turn a-writin' that note and a worse turn by actin' so mean when Granny died, and I come to say I'm right sorry."

"I know ye be, Toby," Preacher Davis said gently. "And I told ye afore, child, there's many ways to grieve. And I reckon ye took yer hurt out a mite different than most folks, Toby, but I knew ye'd come around. Ye got yer granny's blood and ye know Troyline didn't alus take a path most folks took." The preacher's eyes were twinkling and I laughed with him, saying, "Well, Preacher, I got me a strange path to travel too. Ye see, I was so mean to Johnny Joe he's done asked Jamie Marlene to wed him in my place."

"Wal, I'll be, Toby. I ain't never heared that." The preacher seemed puzzled.

"Jamie Marlene told me so herself, Preacher, and her folks done moved in the old Odom place so they could be close to her after her and Johnny Joe's wed. But, Preacher, if I can help it, the only weddin' Johnny Joe is gonna have is mine."

"I know, Toby, 'tis it jist don't seem right for the woman to do the huntin'."

"I don't see the cat-hair why not, Preacher, when she has to live with the game the rest of her born days."

The preacher's eyes laughed again and he scratched his white head, saying, "Ye might be right at that, Toby. Reckon I'm old and have old ways."

"Ye ain't that old, Preacher; 'sides Granny said womenfolks have alus been the catchers where menfolks was concerned. Said womenfolks was born a-knowin' how to trap them. And I jist have to fetch the bait."

"Wal, Toby, ye know sometimes other animals steal the bait ye set out."

"This bait ain't gonna be stole, Preacher," I said. " 'Cause the bait is gonna be me."

"Ye be careful, Toby gal, 'cause it's been knowed fer animals to gobble the bait up and run off."

"Reckon I'll take my chances, Preacher, and be leavin' ye, too. I'll be seein' ye in church Sunday."

"Wal, praise the Lord, Toby, and ye can't go far wrong."

Fat, damp snowflakes were falling as I left the preacher's house, but I didn't care. I was going to see Johnny Joe and the same old warm glow filled me like it used to before Granny died.

Johnny Joe was as usual in the barn. This

time he was putting clean straw down for a newborn calf. When he saw me, he just nodded and he didn't come toward me with smiling eyes the way he always did before.

The light went out of my heart, leaving it cold and bleak like the weather outside. But I kept grinning, for Granny always said ye caught more bees with sugar than with vinegar. She always said a man with hurt feelings was like a rooster with his tail feathers pulled out. I mean, all the strut and cockiness gone. Well, reckon it was up to me to get Johnny Joe some new tail feathers.

"Johnny Joe, I come to say I'm right sorry for the stupid way I acted when Granny went on. Can't rightly say what come over me and reckon it ain't no excuse. But sorry I am."

"Ye done some mighty yellin' and rough talkin', little Toby," Johnny Joe said, coming to lean on the fence near me. I climbed up on the fence where I could reach him. And looking in his eyes I tried to let them say all I couldn't get into words. At first his eyes were hard, then they softened and there was a puzzled, sorta hurt look like he wasn't sure what had happened. And knowing girls like Jamie Marlene, I reckoned he didn't. Not that I was any better, but Johnny Joe was mine.

I reached up, hooked both arms around his neck, and held on when he tried to shake me loose. I plastered my lips on his and kept them there till he was a-hugging instead of pushing me away. After a bit I plumb forgot what I was trying to do to Johnny Joe and started to enjoy myself, figuring if kissing was that good, I was plainly old enough to wed.

Johnny Joe was panting and so was I. Like we was trying to get down each other's throat. His mouth and tongue tasted sweet and I would have melted and run down his leg iffen he hadn't of held me up.

Lord have mercy, if all hugging and kissing was this good, it wasn't no wonder there was bastards in this world. Like me and George, I mean.

It's for sure and a fact I didn't want to be dead like Granny if there was such as this in the world to enjoy. And hair-fire, I couldn't let Jamie Marlene have my Johnny Joe. 'Cause I wanted to wed him so's I could hang on him whenever I wanted. And from the looks of things I'd want to more than once every day.

When we come to ourselves, somebody was trying to get in the other's britches. I don't know if it was me or him or both of us; anyway, Johnny Joe stopped it. His face was red, his eyes glazed, and he was sweating, and reckon I wasn't in no better shape myself; but when Johnny Joe kept saying he was sorry, I let him think the fault was all his.

"I won't hurt ye, little Toby," he said, his big hand trembling as he smoothed my hair. If that was hurt, I wanted to say, "Hurt me, Hurt me!" but knew I'd better be quiet. We leaned against each other in an uneasy peace, wanting more, knowing better.

"Toby girl, this here ain't right. 'Cause since yore Granny died, things have changed." I knew he was going to tell me about Jamie Marlene, so I put my hands across his mouth and, looking lovingly in his eyes, said, "I know, Johnny Joe. I was mean, and 'stead of leaning on ye as I ought, I run ye off, but I'll make it up to ye, you'll see. My Johnny Joe, ye'll see and I reckon fifteen ain't too young to wed neither, though Granny thought a body ought to be older."

Before he could protest, I pressed another kiss on him, wishing I had big tits to rub against him. But as Granny always said, a body had to make do with what the good Lord gave them.

I drew away saying fastlike that I had chores to do and would see him later. I dashed out in the snow fast, hearing him call me and acting like I didn't. I knew he'd be over after chore time and I had me some work cut out before he came. For Johnny Joe would be honor bound to tell me about him being bound by Jamie Marlene.

9

I dashed home through the snow and got a leaping fire going in the fireplace and the cookstove. I drew up water for a bath, and started cooking.

Like all hillfolks, Johnny Joe liked his vittles. For farm people worked hard, from early to late, and food was a treat and a comfort. And I must say, I sorta outdone myself.

I made two chocolate pies with egg whites high and golden brown. I opened a large jar of the beef chunks Granny had canned in the summer, and pouring it in a pot, I added a handful of herbs, onion, and potatoes. I opened a jar of home-canned green beans and made biscuit dough.

The house looked warm and cozy in the fire and coal-oil lamplight, and felt even more so with the smell of baking and good food filling the air.

I bathed in the washtub and put on my gold-yellow dress. I put the biscuits in the oven, and sitting in Granny's rocker before the fireplace, I waited. And it wasn't long until Johnny Joe was knocking at the door. He sniffed the air like a hound scenting coon, saying, "Ye allus dress up at night by yore lonesome, Toby?"

"Jist felt like wearin' the dress Granny got me."

His glance saw the table and looked surprised. "Ye shore cook a lot fer jist ye, Toby."

"Wal, they's times I get mighty hungry,

Johnny Joe. 'Sides, I was ever the one fer bakin'." I pulled the biscuits from the oven, saying, "Ye sit and eat with me, Johnny Joe."

"Toby, I gotta say my say and then I reckon ye might not welcome me at yore table."

I opened my eyes wide and stared up at him, saying, "Why, I swan, Johnny Joe, what ever do ye mean?"

"When yore granny died, ye didn't act like ye keered fer me anymore. And, Toby, ye know a man works hard in these hills and wal, Toby gal, I reckon ye wouldn't know of such things, but a man needs comfort of a lovin' wife. Ye know I love ye, little Toby, and reckon I allus will; but when I thought ye'd lost yore hankerin' fer me, I asked Jamie Marlene to wed." Johnny Joe sputtered to a stop. And sending a silent message for Granny to help me, I allowed myself to slump, little and helpless, in my gold-yellow dress nigh the chocolate pies and hot biscuits. Since there ain't nothing uglier than a bawling woman, I just let a couple of tears roll gentlelike down what I hoped was rosy cheeks and reckoned to myself there was nothing as sneaking than a woman trying to get a man neither.

"Oh, Toby, my little Toby." Johnny Joe moaned. I straightened bravely, tilting my chin, and said in a trembling voice, "I don't blame ye, Johnny Joe. Not a'tall. And I want ye to know I'll alus be yore friend." But I let my lips say "kiss me" and my eyes say "hug me," while I bravely smiled and talked gaily while Johnny Joe stuffed himself, saying something about city gals not cooking good.

After supper I talked on everything I could think of, except Johnny Joe being promised to Jamie Marlene. Every time Johnny Joe would try to tell me how sorry he was, I would lay my hand across his lips, softly as a kiss, and tell him to hush and that it was all my fault anyway.

After he left, promising to be as close friends as we ever were, I stripped off the gold-yellow dress and looked at my small, skinny body, my breasts no bigger than green walnuts. "Yer bait didn't 'mount to much, Toby," I said out loud. "It's a dang good thing ye can cook."

I fell asleep, saying, "Lord, forgive me, but Johnny Joe was mine first. Ye understand, don't Ye, Lord?" And inside me I knew that come the morning I was going to visit Jamie Marlene. Knowing we'd never be friends, but it wouldn't hurt to know what was happening in the enemy camp.

I talked to the Lord again that night. I knew well as could be that I was doing a backhanded thing, but my life wouldn't be worth living without Johnny Joe. And I was sure as shootin' Jamie Marlene would make Johnny Joe unhappy. Johnny Joe needed me. 'Sides, the Lord knew Johnny Joe was mine first. And running folks off when a body was crazy didn't count. Fact of the matter, Johnny Joe ought to have known I didn't mean it. But anybody can take just so much cussing.

Now I think I knew what Granny meant when she said that even the bad times were good. For all my troubles, it was so good to be Toby again, to be feeling. Even if some of the feeling did hurt some. Felt powerful good to like kissing Johnny Joe. I mean, fact of the matter, I reckon I'd kiss his dang head off every time I saw him. Till he forgot all about Jamie Marlene.

I slept, hugging my pillow and thinking this must be what Granny was talking about when she said a woman knew when she was woman grown. And sometimes it came on a body sudden. Reckon mine come on me when Johnny Joe was kissing me in the barn. I felt all tingly alive in places I hardly knew I had before.

I didn't feel so sure of myself when I got to the Odom's place the next day, for Jamie Marlene wore a red dress and had a red ribbon in her hair. That dumb dog of hers had on a red ribbon, too, and I had to admit they was a mighty pretty picture but one that somehow didn't seem to belong in the farm country of the Arkansas hills.

Jamie's mother was a plumb cheerful woman and her pa the same. Ye could tell they doted on their young'un; her being the only one, I reckon. They'd fixed the house up with new paint and colorful wallpaper. There was town-bought rugs on the floors, too. Not home-braided like mine and most of the other folks around.

They insisted I stay for supper, and being neighborly, I said, "Yes," then was sorry I did when Jamie giggled that Johnny Joe was coming, too. I wished I'd of wore my gold-yellow dress; my overalls and brogues shore seemed out of place in a citified house. They insisted I let George come in out of the snow. And he proceeded to make an ass out of himself at once 'cause he wanted Fluffy's red ribbon, too. I finally had to push him down and put my feet on him, feeling like a fool.

Jamie's ma said, "Ye girls jist have a good visit now, while I fix supper." I didn't see how we could visit much, with Jamie a-stealing my man and me having to hold that ass, George, down with both feet.

I don't know how I done it. Smiled, I mean; then Jamie said, "Land sakes, Toby, I'm right glad ye all ain't mad at me fer a-weddin' Johnny Joe. 'Cause I heared ye and him was right thick afore I come along."

So she did know Johnny Joe was mine and she stole him a purpose, I thought, but I smiled at her friendly as could be, and my voice dripped sugar as I said, "Why, I shore ain't mad, Jamie Marlene, 'cause it's a long ways from the askin' to the church."

"Why, whatever do ye mean, Toby?"

I didn't answer but asked, "When is the weddin' to take place, Jamie?"

"Wal, maybe spring, I reckon. That big, ole Johnny Joe is so impatient."

Suddenly I was sick and tired of smiling and sick and tired of being backhanded and sneaking. Planting my feet more firmly on George, I turned and looked Jamie Marlene square in the eye and said, "Jamie Marlene, Johnny Joe is my man. Alus has been; alus will be. He jist turned to ye 'cause I was rotten mean over Granny's passing on. And I reckon ye had a lot to do with that. Now, I ain't blamin' ye none fer that 'cause womenfolks is jist natural-born sneaky where menfolks are concerned, but I'm a-tellin' ye plain out, ye ain't a-gettin' Johnny Joe."

All the giggles and silliness was gone from Jamie Marlene's face, and I wondered why I ever thought her dumb and silly anyways. She said, cold as ice, "Toby, ye done lost out. I wanted Johnny Joe for my husband the first time I seen him and I don't give up easy."

"I don't know what givin' up means, Jamie Marlene, but I might iffen I thought ye really loved Johnny Joe. A forever love, I mean. But I've knowed Johnny Joe a long spell and ye jist ain't the right sort for him."

"We'll see about that, Toby. We'll jist see!"

"Jamie, has Johnny Joe ever spanked you?"

"Lord, no!" she squealed.

"Wal, there ye go. Ye see, he did me, but it was 'cause he keered so much about me. He was a-tryin' to get me to do right."

"I don't see that has anything to do with nothin', Toby."

Before I could say anything else, Johnny Joe tapped on the door.

10

Johnny Joe looked plumb surprised to see me sitting beside Jamie. His face turned sorta red, and I felt like a ginny hen next to a peacock.

Jamie Marlene turned back to her giggling self. Her ma fluttered around, putting food on the table, and her pa just sit, saying, "Humph, humph," once in a while, looking at his womenfolk, proud as could be.

When supper was called, I had to push George out on the porch and slam the door on him.

I sat on one side of Johnny Joe and Jamie on the other. I don't know what made me do it. I mean, after telling Jamie I was going to be honest and open with her about courting Johnny Joe. Maybe it was 'cause of the way Jamie Marlene was giggling close to him and getting closer, and Johnny Joe thought her such a lady, I sneered to myself. I loosed one of my heavy shoes off and figured if I twisted my leg around just right I could rub Johnny Joe's leg next to Jamie Marlene and he'd think it was her being hussyfied.

It nigh broke my leg getting it twisted so far, but the pain was worth it. At the first touch of my toes that I hoped felt like fingers, Johnny Joe went stiff as a board, and his eyes sorta bugged and his already red face got more so.

"I declare to goodness, Johnny Joe, yer blushin' somethin' fierce," Jamie Marlene simpered. "Reckon it's 'cause yer sittin' betwixt yore intended and yore old flame." When she giggled again, I gave another easy rub with my toes, nearly to the fork in his britches. Johnny Joe choked and pushed his chair back, still coughing.

"Land sakes, boy, what's wrong?" Jamie's ma fluttered.

"B-b-bone," Johnny Joe stuttered, leaving her with a blank look. Then she said, "Son, there ain't no bones in a sweet 'tater."

"Jist went down the wrong way, I reckon," Johnny Joe muttered. That was when I realized something was powerful wrong. When Johnny Joe pushed his chair back, it had sent my naked foot flying to land on the old pa's leg under the table. And watching Johnny Joe, I had absentmindly kept rubbing, only it was the old man's leg. I sent a scared look at him, feeling like a fool, and he was grinning like one. I yanked my foot back like a shot, and from the look on his face I knew there was some beller left in the old bull yet!

Somehow I got my shoe back on, but now my face was red as Johnny Joe's. Reckon I got repaid for my sins fast that time. I said a quick "thank ye for the supper" and that I had to rush home and do the chores. For I had rather they think I didn't have good manners, or good sense, for that matter, by not offering to help with the dishes, than look at that grinning old man again.

Johnny Joe said he best go with me, for the snowstorm was worse. Jamie Marlene didn't want him to and pouted a little. But she was smart enough not to get too bossy till she had him hog-tied.

We was halfway home before the red seeped out of Johnny Joe's face. I was glad in more ways than one that he'd come with me, for the wind had risen to a loud howl and kept knocking me offen my feet, and Johnny Joe kept picking me up till he was nigh carrying me.

George ran on ahead, paying us no mind, for he was still holding a grudge at me for not letting him steal Fluffy's red ribbon.

When we got to the house we built up the fire, then fought the hard-spitting snow to the barn lot to do the evening chores.

When we finished, we were both nigh froze and was feeling the supper we'd all but missed at Jamie's.

Johnny Joe put a pot of coffee on, and I pushed the pot of pinto beans on the front of the stove to heat and fried Johnny corn cakes to eat with them.

When we was through eating, we took our hot, sweet, milky coffee to the fireplace and sat on the floor, taking our shoes off to warm our bare toes.

"Toby, I want to talk with ye," Johnny Joe said, looking softly down at me with his blue, shy eyes, saying, "Toby, I love ye, wrong or not. A-waitin' fer ye to get over yore granny's passin', I reckon I was powerful hurt 'cause I thought ye'd turned on me. And wal, truth to tell, it seemed Jamie Marlene was alus around a-braggin' on me. Sorta pumpin' me up in places a man needs. She alus smelled good and was nice to look at, but, little Toby, it was ye I wanted, and alus will. And when I seen ye so little and small sittin' beside Jamie Marlene on the couch, wal, I knew I could never marry Jamie. I know to break off with her is no gentlemanly thing to do, but it would be worse to wed her without love. Yer my gal, Toby. Ain't never been, nor never will be, no other. I'll help ye keep this farm up and in a year or so when yer right shore yer're woman growed, then we'll wed."

I threw my arms around Johnny Joe's neck and loved all I wanted to before he pushed me away, saying, "Now, Toby gal, ye know we can't have a whole lot of that thar carryin' on 'cause yore granny trusted us. And truth to tell, ye jist got to get more top and bottom afore yer woman growed."

"I know yer right, Johnny Joe, and I'll get bigger. It's jist that I shore love hugs and kisses."

"I do too, Toby, but, wal, everything in its season, as the Good Book says."

"I can wait, Johnny Joe," I said softly, looking in his kind, happy face. My heart was flooding with love for my big, gentle Johnny Joe. I'd never ever shut him out of my life again, no matter what.

Suddenly I noticed Johnny Joe's face turning red again and he stuttered, "To— Toby, ye know tonight at supper that Jamie gal played with my leg."

"Like this?" I giggled, stretching out my toes and rubbing them up and down his leg. Johnny Joe stared at me, then began to laugh; grabbing my foot he pulled me across the floor, me squealing and giggling. And George danced around us on his hind legs.

After Johnny Joe left, I sang as I cleaned the dishes, dreaming of when me and Johnny Joe's young'uns filled the house. And one of the girls would be named Troyline. She'd have red-apple cheeks and snapping black eyes. She'd be a witch who knew all about herbs, but more about people.

I shook myself out of my dream and went to sit on Granny's bed, dragging George up with me. I thought about Granny and how she was right. That most things died, but love never did. Bits and parts of Granny would always be with me—the knowledge of herbs she'd taught me and the helping of other folks, even when you didn't like them. There was strength in caring. The love of God and man, she'd taught me, also the love of hard work, the feel of sweat drenching your body, the good of cleanness, and not even to mind our poorness. For deep hunger made even the plainest food taste like nectar.

I stretched across the bed and it suddenly seemed I could feel myself start to grow. Flipping over on my belly, I reached for Granny's old, worn Bible and it fell open to the chapter she most loved. The one I'd read and teach my children, and as I read, the love Granny had give me for all my years settled around me like a warm blanket with no rough spots or hurt.

I CORINTHIANS
Chapter 13

Though I speak with the tongues of men and of angels, and have not charity, I am become as sounding brass, or a tinkling cymbal.

2. And though I have the gift of prophecy, and understand all mysteries, and all knowledge; and though I have all faith, so that I could remove mountains, and have not charity, I am nothing.

3. And though I bestow all my goods to feed the poor, and though I give my body to be burned, and have not charity, it profiteth me nothing.

4. Charity suffereth long, and is kind; charity envieth not; charity vaunteth not itself, is not puffed up,

5. Doth not behave itself unseemly, seeketh not her own, is not easily provoked, thinketh no evil;

6. Rejoiceth not in iniquity, but rejoiceth in the truth;

7. Beareth all things, believeth all

things, hopeth all things, endureth all things.

8. Charity never faileth: but whether there be prophecies, they shall fail; whether there be tongues, they shall cease; whether there be knowledge, it shall vanish away.

9. For we know in part, and we prophesy in part.

10. But when that which is perfect is come, then that which is in part shall be done away.

11. When I was a child, I spake as a child, I understood as a child, I thought as a child; but when I became a man, I put away childish things.

12. For now we see through a glass darkly; but then face to face: now I

know in part; but then shall I know even as also I am known.

13. And now abideth faith, hope, charity, these three; but the greatest of these is charity.

ROBBIE BRANSCUM bases her stories on her own life: "I was born on a farm somewhere on the outskirts of Big Flat, Arkansas. I went to school in a one-room schoolhouse at Red Oak, where at that time the eighth grade was as high as a person aimed. I can remember the mental hunger for books, and a book was something to cherish, to be read over and over.

"I still like to raise my own vegetables and dream of a small farm, a creek, a moon as big as a summer sky, the far-off bay of hounds, running fox and coon, and my Arkansas hills that never quite leave one's blood."

Robbie Branscum now lives and writes in California.

10057

South Shore High School
Port Wing, Wisconsin

South Shore High School
Port Wing, Wisconsin